Everyone was hot.

The children wanted to
go swimming.

Dad said, "No!"

Biff got the paddling pool.

Kipper filled it with water.

Chip pushed Biff in the water.

He grabbed the hose.

8

They had a water fight.

Mum got wet.

"Stop it!" said Dad.

Dad got a bucket of water.

He chased Chip.

Dad threw the water at Chip.

Oh no!

"Sorry!" said Dad.